# The further adventures of the little mouse trapped in a book

## STORY AND PICTURES
## BY MONIQUE FELIX

© 1983 MONIQUE FELIX Éditions TOURNESOL-CARABOSSE S.A.
1025, SAINT-SULPICE SWITZERLAND
A STAR & ELEPHANT BOOK
FROM THE GREEN TIGER PRESS
LA JOLLA, CALIFORNIA 92038
ISBN 0-88138-009-1